Witch*Wendy

Books by Alex Gutteridge

Witch Wendy

1. Cats and Hats

2. Broom Broom!

3. Cat Tricks

Witch⋆Wendy

Broom Broom!

Alex Gutteridge

Illustrated by Annabel Hudson

MACMILLAN CHILDREN'S BOOKS

For my mother

First published 2002 by Macmillan Children's Books Ltd
a division of Macmillan Publishers Limited
20 New Wharf Road, London N1 9RR
Basingstoke and Oxford
www.panmacmillan.com

Associated companies throughout the world

ISBN 0 330 39851 2

3 5 7 9 8 6 4 2

A CIP catalogue record for this book is available from
the British Library.

Typeset by Macmillan Publishers Limited
Printed and bound in Great Britain by Mackays of Chatham plc, Kent

Chapter One

Witch Wendy couldn't believe it, her broomstick had broken down! Wendy tried everything: she chanted all the broomstick breakdown spells in the book; she soaked it in flying ointment; and finally, she whacked it with her wand. Nothing worked. The broomstick was kaput!

"What am I going to do?" she wailed at Snowflake, her cat. "The Broomstick Race is only two nights away and I haven't got anything to fly on!"

Snowflake sighed. He handed Wendy her hat and picked up the broken broomstick.

"We'll just have to go to the garage to get it mended," he said.

"But how will we get there?" asked Wendy.

"Walk, of course," replied Snowflake.

"Witches aren't *meant* to walk," Wendy scowled.

"Cats aren't *meant* to fly," said Snowflake, "but every night I'm catapulted into the sky. Now, are you coming or not?"

Wendy sulked all the way to the Broom Broom Garage while Snowflake pulled the broomstick.

There was a big silver sign above the

garage. It read: *We'll put the Vroom back in your broom*.

"I hope he means that," said Wendy.

Mr Revit, the repair man, looked at the broomstick and pursed his lips.

"Has it been in a crash?" he asked.

"One or two," murmured Snowflake.

"Nothing major." Wendy smiled her most bewitching smile. "Just the odd little prang."

Mr Revit didn't look convinced.

"It'll take a week," he said.

"A week!" Wendy shrieked. "I haven't got a week. The Witches' Annual Broomstick Race is on Midsummer's Eve. That's the night after tomorrow!"

"We'll have to buy another broomstick," said Snowflake.

Mr Revit shook his head.

"It's been worse than Halloween in here for the last couple of days. I haven't got any broomsticks left."

"Well, that's it then," said Wendy as they walked home. "I can't take part in the Broomstick Race."

"Look on the bright side," said Snowflake,

secretly quite pleased. "At least we won't come last again."

"But we'll have to sit with the elves and the fairies and the weak and wimpy witches," whined Wendy. "Then there's Rosemary, Primrose and Harriet. You know what they'll say."

"What?" yawned Snowflake.

"If you don't take part in the broomstick race, it's a whole year until you can show your face."

"So we wouldn't be able to go out for a year?" Snowflake asked.

"Only on our own," said Wendy. "But we wouldn't be allowed to mix with other witches – or their cats."

Snowflake pulled his whiskers and twanged them back into place. He thought of Witch Harriet's cat, Sable, and he felt his legs go all wobbly. Then he thought of Witch Rosemary's cat, Coalface. Coalface would have a whole year to use his charms on Sable.

Snowflake suddenly
made up his mind.

"Of course you must
take part in the race,"
he said.

"But how?" asked Wendy.

"Witches don't have to use broomsticks,
do they?" asked Snowflake.

"Well, no," said Wendy.

"Witches sometimes use other forms of
transport, don't they?" asked Snowflake.

"Well, yes," said Wendy.

"Then we'll find something else to fly
on," said Snowflake.

Witch Wendy picked Snowflake up and

kissed the top of his head.

"Snowflake," she said. "I'm so lucky to have you. I know you always have my best interests at heart."

Chapter Two

Wendy and Snowflake had nearly reached home when they saw three shadowy shapes hurtling through the sky.

"Watch out, witches about!" warned Snowflake.

Wendy hurried up the garden path. Something smelly and scary swooped down and landed in front of her.

"Rosemary!" Wendy took a step backwards. "You startled me!"

"Hee! Hee! Hee!" cackled Rosemary. "That's what witches are meant to do Wendy, or have you forgotten?"

"Hee! Hee! Hee!" echoed Primrose and Harriet, as they hovered over the hedge.

"Of ... of course not," stuttered Wendy. "It's just that I don't like scaring people very much."

"Pah!" spat Rosemary. Her eyes narrowed and turned deep pink like slivers of beetroot. "Wendy, why are you a walking witch? Where's your broomstick?"

"It's … it's giving me a bit of bother," Wendy stammered.

"Are you going to miss the Broomstick Race?" Rosemary leered and pushed her beaky nose close to Wendy's face. "What a pity."

"An absolute cat-astrophe," crowed Coalface.

Snowflake arched his back and swished his tail.

"I don't suppose anyone's got a spare broomstick?" Wendy asked.

"Well—" began Harriet.

"Borrowing broomsticks is against the Flyway Code," Rosemary ranted. "You'll just have to sit on the skyline, Wendy, with the other wimpy witches."

"Oh no, she won't," growled Snowflake. "It's all sorted out. I've found a replacement broomstick."

"What?"exclaimed Rosemary, Primrose and Harriet.

"What?" whispered Wendy.

"Really?" sneered Rosemary. "I expect it's a garden spade or a mop? They don't fly at all well. It'll take you a year to finish the race!"

Her horrible cackle made the moon quiver and the stars shrink into the night sky.

"It's neither of those," said Snowflake.

"Tell me what it is," Rosemary roared. "I want to know."

"You'll have to wait and see," said Snowflake. "But it's even better than a broomstick."

"Better than a broomstick?" cackled Primrose and Harriet, almost falling into the hedge they laughed so much.

"I'm so-o-o-o scared," sneered Rosemary. "Positively squirming on my seat!"

"Cowering in our cloaks!" agreed Primrose.

"Fretting from our foreheads to our feet!" sang Harriet.

"And so you should be!" shouted Snowflake, as he dragged Wendy into the house. "You should be three worried witches," and he slammed the front door shut.

Chapter Three

"So," whispered Wendy as soon as the witches were out of eavesdropping distance, "what is it then?"

"What's what?" asked Snowflake, putting down his toothbrush and climbing into his basket.

"What is it that's even better than a

broomstick?" Wendy sighed.

"Oh, that," yawned Snowflake. "I don't know yet, but we'll think of something."

"Well?" asked Wendy after breakfast the next evening. "Have you thought of something?"

"I'm working on it," said Snowflake. "You can't rush a genius. Have you noticed all these cobwebs around the ceiling?"

"Witches' houses are meant to be full of cobwebs," murmured Wendy.

"They make me sneeze," said Snowflake.

He prised open a cupboard door with his paw and took out some cleaning materials.

"That's it!" shouted Wendy, jumping up, spilling her tea and tossing her toast and marmalade into the air. "You are a genius, Snowflake!"

"I am?" queried Snowflake.

Wendy skipped to the cupboard.

"This is what we'll use: a feather duster.

It's the right shape, it's light and it'll glide through the air like ..."

"... like a bird breaking the speed limit," grinned Snowflake.

"Let's try it out," said Wendy, rubbing some flying ointment along the handle. "Hop on the back."

Snowflake rushed to get his crash helmet and settled on the pink, yellow and blue feathers. He tried to get comfortable while Wendy concocted a spell.

"Feather duster, rise to the ceiling,
Flap your tail
and send the cobwebs reeling."

The feather duster rose slowly into the air and glided around the room, flicking at the cobwebs.

Snowflake started to giggle. He started to wiggle. The feather duster started to wobble.

"Sit still," commanded Wendy.

"I can't help it," Snowflake gasped.

The feather duster rocked violently from side to side. It reared up like a horse and then charged headlong into the fireplace.

Wendy was covered in soot and Snowflake had a splinter up his nose.

"Sorry," Snowflake sniffed. "I don't think that will work."

"Not if you don't sit still," snapped Wendy.

"I couldn't. The feathers were tickling my bottom," said Snowflake.

"We'll just have to think of something else," said Wendy.

Snowflake scraped the marmalade and toast off the rug and put it in the bin.

"It's a bit obvious," he said, "but I don't suppose you've considered a flying carpet?"

"We could try it, I suppose," said Wendy, whipping the rug out from underneath the table. "We'll take it outside, where there's more room."

Wendy put the rug in the middle of the lawn and sat down on it.

Snowflake stood at the back and dug his

claws into the carpet.

"Carpet, rise into the air,

And up to the clouds if you dare!"

Nothing happened. Wendy tapped it with her wand. She put a blob of flying ointment at each corner. She tried again.

"Carpet, rise above the ground,

Or in the dustbin you'll be found!"

The rug rose a few inches above the grass and hovered.

"O-o-o-h!" wailed Snowflake as the carpet crumpled and crinkled in the middle. "I'm going to fall off!"

"Nonsense," said Wendy. "It's just a question of getting used to it, that's all."

"Carpet, head for the nearest tree,
Let's see how quick you
can really be!"

The rug jerked towards a large oak tree.

It was heading straight for the tree trunk.

"Help!" wailed Snowflake.

"Stop!" Wendy commanded the carpet.

The carpet didn't take any notice.

"Jump!" shouted Snowflake.

Wendy and Snowflake jumped and sploshed straight into the garden pond. The carpet crashed into the tree and slid to the ground like a stunned snake.

"It's hopeless!" Wendy spluttered. "We can't take part in the broomstick race unless one of us has a marvellous, magical idea."

Chapter Four

It was Midsummer's Eve. The weather was perfect for broomstick racing. The sky was as clear as a crystal ball, with a helpful breeze to blow them along – but Wendy was glum. She hadn't found anything suitable to fly on.

"Cooo-eee," a witchy voice called down Wendy's chimney.

"What do you want, Rosemary?" Wendy sighed.

"Are you ready for the Broomstick Race?" asked Rosemary in her sneakiest, meanest voice.

"She knows I'm not," Wendy said to Snowflake. "She just wants to gloat."

Snowflake raced over to the windows and pulled the curtains across as Primrose and Harriet pressed their warty noses against the glass.

He just caught a glimpse of Sable's glossy fur and green eyes. She looked beautiful in the moonlight.

"See you next year, dear," cackled

Rosemary. She circled the chimney pot and blew down it so hard that Wendy's fire went out.

"We'll see you sooner than that, or I'm not a cat, *dear*," Snowflake wheezed up the chimney.

"Piffle!" Rosemary spat, and the three witches flew off in a frantic flurry.

"Who needs a fire extinguisher with Rosemary around?" Wendy coughed through clouds of smoke.

Suddenly Snowflake flung his paws around her and licked her face.

"You're a wonder-witch! Put your racing clothes on. Hurry, or we'll be late."

"Hold on, Snowflake," Wendy sobbed, "there's a small problem. We haven't got anything to ride on."

Snowflake whipped the bright red fire extinguisher off the wall.

"We have now," he said. "Just think of this as a supersonic broomstick. Rosemary will be mean with envy. Trust me."

Snowflake checked his watch. The race was due to start at midnight – they had ten minutes to get there.

Wendy put on her traffic-cone hat, turned on the light and sat at the front of the fire extinguisher.

"Let's have a spell," said Snowflake.

"I don't know any fire-extinguisher spells," said Wendy.

"Make one up then," said Snowflake.

"Something like:

Fire extinguisher travel into the night,
Take us to the race with all your might."

Snowflake rubbed the flying ointment on the metal container.

Wendy tapped it three times with her wand.

The extinguisher rumbled inside, it juddered, then it rose into the air and hovered for a moment in the doorway.

"It's not going to work," said Wendy.

"It's just warming up, that's all," said Snowflake.

As soon as he said this, the extinguisher began to taxi down the garden path. Then it thundered up the road and launched itself towards the clouds.

They were at the race in eight minutes. Everyone was lined up at the starting star. Wendy edged in next to Rosemary.

"What on earth … ?"

The waiting witches stared at the supersonic broomstick.

"You can't be serious," hooted Harriet.

"It's so embarrassing," bawled Primrose.

"It must be against the rules," hissed Rosemary.

The Chief Wizard came over. He inspected the supersonic broomstick very carefully.

Wendy could hardly breathe. If she was disqualified here, in front of everyone, she would never, ever be able to show her face again.

The wizard stroked his beard and muttered to himself under his moustache. Snowflake looked at the starting star and made a wish. Then he nuzzled his nose against Wendy's back.

The wizard shook his head several times. It wasn't a good omen.

Chapter Five

"There's nothing in the rule book to say it isn't allowed," mused the wizened wizard.

"Well, there should be," snapped Rosemary. "I shall re-write the book for next year."

"You may take part," said the wizard to

Wendy. He bowed deeply.

"Yes-s-s!" said Wendy and Snowflake, clasping hand and paw together.

"It's disgraceful," spluttered Primrose.

"Such a let down," Harriet jeered.

"I expect you'll come last again," snarled Rosemary, pushing to the front with her superb stick. "It's not exactly streamlined, is it?"

"As long as I finish the race, I don't mind," said Wendy.

"Pah!" spat Rosemary. "Everyone wants to win."

Wendy shrank back into the swarm of witches and waited for the wizard to light the Fantastic Firework to start the race.

"Ready, witches," warned the wizard. "Steady, cats, GO!"

The firework soared into space and exploded in a torrent of tiny orange sparks.

Rosemary got off to a flying start, launching herself towards the ground. The sparks rained down on to her cloak like a sprinkling of glitter. The witches nosedived after her.

Wendy and Snowflake whizzed over woods, swept across streams and raced along empty roads. For once there weren't any mishaps. Wendy felt wonderful.

Even Snowflake was quite enjoying himself.

"Only one more lap to go," he called, after they'd been around the course six times.

Rosemary was out in front, whipping her broomstick with her wand. She was travelling so fast that she seemed to glow in the dark.

Wendy leaned forwards and whispered into the wind.

"Fire extinguisher,
we need to be quick,
Just like a
supersonic broomstick!"

"Mia-ow," cried Snowflake as the fire extinguisher lurched away from the other witches.

It sped past Primrose and Harriet and skimmed through the sky towards Rosemary.

Wendy and Snowflake pulled up alongside. Rosemary was furious.

"Go away," she screeched. "You shouldn't be up here. You must be cheating."

"I told you to watch out," said Snowflake. He sniffed the air. He could smell burning. Little plumes of smoke spiralled out from under Rosemary's cloak. The broomstick was making a crackling, crunching noise.

"You'd better slow down, Rosemary!" called Snowflake. "Your broomstick's over-heating."

"Nonsense," stormed Rosemary. "I'm not going to fall for any of your cat tricks."

"We're nearly there!" Wendy called excitedly to Snowflake. "I can see the

Finishing Well. There are two frogs either side of it waving flags. It's just the other side of those trees."

The other witches were catching up. They whooped and yelled and pointed with their gnarled fingers.

"Fire!" they shrieked. "Rosemary's on fire!"

Snowflake looked at the back of Rosemary's broomstick. Flames were starting to unfurl around the bottom of her cloak.

Coalface was flapping at the flames with his paws.

"Stop!" he mewed at Rosemary. "My bottom's getting hot!"

"Not until we've won," snapped Rosemary.

As they dived in amongst the trees Wendy took the lead. Rosemary was hot on her tail. She bumped the back of the fire extinguisher.

"Let me through, Wendy!"

Wendy zig-zagged from side to side. She weaved up and down.

Rosemary couldn't get past. She gave one last huge thump into the back of Wendy's supersonic broomstick. Wendy lurched forwards and clung to the handle at the front of the fire extinguisher.

Snowflake thudded into her back.

There was a rumbling from inside the extinguisher. It shuddered. It juddered. It felt as if it was going to explode. A jet of foam shot out from the hose at the side and streamed backwards through the air.

It splooshed all over Rosemary and Coalface.

"This is cheating," spluttered Rosemary, trying to see where she was going.

But Wendy didn't hear. She was trying to control the supersonic broomstick. It rolled to the right. Then it lurched to the left.

Wendy and Snowflake slid and slithered on the foam-splattered seat.

Branches battered against Wendy's hat.

Twigs tugged at Snowflake's tail.

"We're going to crash," Wendy shouted.
"Jump!"

"Here we go again," sighed Snowflake.

Chapter Six

Wendy was buried under some brambles. Snowflake spotted the flashing light on top of her hat.

"Out you come," he said pulling the prickly stems away with his paws.

"Oh, Snowflake," Wendy sobbed. "We'd so nearly won the race. Now we'll have come last again. I can't bear it!"

"Never mind," said Snowflake. "It's the taking part that counts."

Wendy hauled herself up. She was covered in scratches, her flying cloak was torn to shreds and she'd lost one of her favourite red shoes.

In the distance Wendy and Snowflake heard clapping and cackling.

"Let's go home," said Snowflake.

"We've got to finish the race," said Wendy. "Those are the rules. I know they'll all laugh, but Rosemary will never let me forget if I don't even get to the Finishing Well."

Snowflake thought of Rosemary covered in foam. He sniggered.

Then he thought how cross she would be and he shivered.

"Are you sure?" said Snowflake. He looked at his messy coat. "Think of all the catty remarks I'll get from Coalface and Sable and Nightshade when they see me looking like this."

But Wendy wasn't listening. She was already picking her way through the undergrowth in the direction of the witches' whooping.

Snowflake tried to tidy himself up with a quick lick and then he followed her out of the trees towards the other witches.

Two foamy figures stood by the Finishing Well. The Chief Wizard handed over the winner's cauldron to the one with the pointy hat.

Suddenly, the watching witches were eerily silent.

"Is that Rosemary?" Wendy asked Snowflake.

"I'm afraid so," said Snowflake.

"What happened to her? Oh, dear, it wasn't anything to do with us, was it?"

"I was going to mention that," Snowflake fidgeted.

"She looks furious," whispered Wendy.

Underneath the white foam Rosemary's skin glowed a livid green. Her eyes blazed red and her tongue darted in and out like a lizard.

"Wendy!" Rosemary growled, spitting foam everywhere. "Come here!"

Wendy tiptoed towards Rosemary.

"I don't know what to say," she started. "You are the most in … in …"

"… incredible?" prompted Snowflake.

"No!" raged Rosemary.

"… intelligent?" said Snowflake helpfully.

"NO!" screamed Rosemary hurling the cauldron to the ground.

"you are absolutely in …"

"… ingenious," said the Chief Wizard. "That is what I think our winner is trying to say. Am I right?"

Rosemary froze.

She made a whistling noise like a kettle coming to the boil, and then she nodded.

It was a very tiny nod but everyone saw it.

"Ingenious?" Wendy gasped. "Me?"

"You lost the race so you could save Rosemary and Coalface," said Harriet.

"*So* generous," purred Sable.

"I did?" said Wendy.

"You did," said Snowflake, nipping the back of her leg.

"If you hadn't been flying that fire extinguisher, I dread to think what would have happened," said Primrose.

"The sparks from the starting firework landed in Rosemary's cloak and began to smoulder …" Harriet said.

"... until they burst into fierce flames," continued Primrose.

"... and singed my whiskers," interrupted Coalface. "I've lost all my looks."

"Three chants for Wendy!" praised the witches.

"A cluster of catcalls for Snowflake!" called Sable.

"And I think Rosemary has something to give you," said Harriet, "to show how grateful she is."

Rosemary scowled.

She stamped her foot.

She pouted her lips.

Then she pushed the winner's cauldron

into Wendy's arms.

"Oh, I can't accept this," said Wendy.

"Yes, you can," said Snowflake. "We'll scratch your name here underneath Rosemary's. By the way," he flashed his eyes at Sable, "I don't suppose anyone can offer us a lift home?"

Later, Snowflake lay in his basket dreaming of Sable. Wendy danced around the room clutching the winner's cauldron.

"Snowflake," she said, "can I ask you something?"

"Fire away," said Snowflake, lazily opening one eye.

"Do you think Rosemary will be a bit nicer to me because I stopped her going up in smoke?"

"Now that," giggled Snowflake, "is the burning question!"